Thanksgiving at OBAACHAN'S

JANET MITSUI BROWN

Library of Congress Cataloging-in-Publication Data

Mitsui Brown, Janet, 1947-
Thanksgiving at Obaachan's / Written & Illustrated by
Janet Mitsui Brown —1st ed.
            p.   cm.

Summary:
A Japanese American girl describes Thanksgiving
at her Grandmother's house.

ISBN No. 1-879965-07-0
1. Japanese Americans — Fiction.
2. Thanksgiving— Fiction.
3. Grandmothers—Fiction.
I. Title

PZ7.M69957Th   1994
[E]—dc20

                93-43933
                CIP
                AC

This is a New Book, Written and Illustrated
Especially for Polychrome Books
First Edition, May 1994

Designed, produced and published by
Polychrome Publishing Corporation
4509 North Francisco Avenue,
Chicago, Illinois 60625-3808
(773) 478-4455 Fax: (773) 478-0786

Editorial Director, Sandra S. Yamate
Art Director, Heather Mark Chen
Production Coordinator, Brian M. Witkowski

Printed in Hong Kong
By O. G. Printing Productions Ltd.
10 9 8 7 6 5 4 3 2

ISBN 1-879965-07-0

To my husband Roger and daughter Tani, for their contagious spirit,

ongoing encouragement and love, and to my father Sat and mother Aki,

for the many Thanksgiving memories that served as inspiration for this book.

I stepped onto the dusty driveway as soon as our car stopped and headed straight for the sounds of laughter and familiar smells. Thanksgiving had finally arrived!

I reached the battered wooden stairs and made my way inside.

We were at Obaachan's house.

Everywhere I looked I saw old used wood. I slipped

off my shoes and placed them neatly by the door.

As I tip-toed into the house, the floors squeaked

and groaned. I made my way to the first bedroom,

peeked in, and I saw her sitting on her bed, looking out the

window. I knocked on the door and she turned and smiled at me.

As I hugged her, I gazed at the familiar flowered pattern embossed on her cotton dress. It felt right.

I saw her butsudan on her dresser out of the corner of my eye, and the photograph of my late Ojiichan in front of it. I breathed in the musty sweet and smokey fragrance that floated from the thin, black, burning sticks nestled in sand.

But I began to cough. "Gomen-nasai."

I didn't know what she said but she pointed to the burning sticks. I started

to cough again, and nodded. She quickly put them out in the sand.

Then we looked at each other and smiled. She doesn't speak English, and I don't speak Japanese. But we talk to each other.

I could hear voices drifting in from the next room. Everyone was talking and laughing at once about Christmas. But I could tell Obaachan had other things on her mind.

I followed her as she walked into the kitchen. The aroma of the cooking turkey and the warmth of the room made me feel content. I spied white rice bubbling on the stove and noticed that the food steamed windows as it cooked. I suddenly realized that I was weak with hunger.

She handed me something.

"Kamaboko," she said.

I took a bite.

"It tastes like fish," I said.

She put her hands together and wiggled them, and then she said, "Fish?"

I nodded.

Her head bobbed as she laughed,

"Ah, sakana."

I spied a triangular riceball covered with black seaweed. I looked at her.

"Onigiri dozo."

I didn't know what she said, so I shrugged.

"Eat?" I asked.

She smiled and gave it to me.

As I took a bite I saw a red plum hidden inside.

I made a face.

"Karai?" she asked.

I nodded and said, "Tart."

"Tart," she repeated. Then she made a funny face.

I nodded.

She handed me a paper napkin, but it stuck

to my fingers because of the sticky rice.

We looked at each other and laughed.

She pointed to the dining room, bowing slightly.

"Dozo." Time to eat.

My mom and dad, my brothers, my aunties, uncles and cousins,

all sat down around the massive table. "Dozo," Obaachan said to me,

gesturing to the special seat next to her. My heart was pounding,

and I could feel my face flush. I had the seat of honor.

As I looked around me, all I could see was food. I could see the leg of the roast turkey in back of the platter of stuffing, and I could hear my stomach growl as the butter melted on the mashed potatoes in front of me.

Out of the corner of my eye I spied pumpkin pie, my auntie's crunchy oatmeal cookies, and my favorite pink and white striped rice cakes, omanju. I decided to start with olives. When no one was looking, I put five of them on my fingers.

Then I heard a clicking sound and saw Obaachan putting turkey on my plate with her ohashi. She saw my fingers and I thought I saw her eyes twinkle but she didn't say a word. Instead, "Gohan?"

Rice, of course.

"With gravy please. And tsukemono." I pointed to the Japanese pickles

sitting on the table, "The yellow ones." She added peas. Yuk.

When all our plates were full, Obaachan sat down

and picked up her ohashi. "Itadakimasu."

It was time to eat.

After dinner I sat on her lap and listened to the chatter and cheerful banter in the room. The sounds of sipping tea made me sleepy. It was my favorite time, Thanksgiving at Obaachan's.

Glossary

Butsudan [boot´·su·don]: Family altar

Dozo [dō´·zō]: Please

Gohan [gō·hăn´]: Rice

Gomen-nasai [gō´·měn nă·sī´]: Excuse me

Hashi (or Ohashi) [ō·hă´·shē]: Chopsticks

Itadakimasu [ē´·tă·dă´·kē·măs]: Let us eat

Kamaboku [kă·mă·bō´·kŭ]: Fish cake

Karai [kă·rī´]: Tart

Manju (or Omanju) [ō·măn´·jū]: Sweet rice cake

Nigiri (or Onigiri) [ō·nĭ´·gĭ·rē]: Riceball

Obaachan [ō·bă´·ă·chăn]: Grandmother

Ojiichan [ō·jē´·ē·chăn]: Grandfather

Sakana [să´·kă·nă]: Fish

Tsukemono [tsū´·kě·mō·nō]: Pickled vegetables

About Polychrome

Founded in 1990, Polychrome Publishing Corporation is an independent press located in Chicago, Illinois, producing children's books for a multicultural market. Polychrome books introduce characters and illustrate situations with which children of all colors can readily identify. They are designed to promote racial, ethnic, cultural and religious tolerance and understanding. We live in a multicultural world. We at Polychrome Publishing Corporation believe that our children need a balanced multicultural education if they are to thrive in that world. Polychrome books can help create that balance.

Acknowledgments

Polychrome Publishing Corporation appreciates the encouragement and help received from Christopher A. Chen, Michael and Kay Janis, Irene Cualoping, Gene Honda, Yvonne Lau, Ngoan Le, Rebecca Lederhouse, Lee Maglaya, Ashraf Manji, Gene Mayeda, Calvin Manshio and Peggy C. Wallace, Kyosik Oh, Sam and Harue Ozaki, Sandra R. Otaka, Lynn Watson, Philip Wong, Mitchell and Laura Witkowski, George and Vicki Yamate, Kiyo Yoshimura, Kay Kawaguchi and the Staff of the Chicago Shimpo, the Chicago Chapter of the Japanese American Citizens League (JACL), and the Japanese American Service Committee (JASC) as well as the continuing interest and support of the Asian American community.

Other Books from Polychrome Publishing Corporation

Char Siu Bao Boy
ISBN 1-879965-00-3

Written by Sandra S. Yamate and illustrated by Joyce MW Jenkin, this story introduces us to Charlie, a Chinese American boy who loves eating his favorite ethnic food for lunch. His friends find his eating preferences strange. Charlie succumbs to peer pressure but misses eating his char siu bao. Find out how he learns to balance assimilation and cultural preservation. 32 pages hardbound (with color illustrations). *Recommended by the State of Hawaii Department of Education.*

Ashok By Any Other Name
ISBN 1-879965-01-1

Written by Sandra S. Yamate and illustrated by Janice Tohinaka. This story is about Ashok, an Indian American boy who wishes he had a more "American" name and the mishaps he experiences as he searches for the perfect name for himself. 36 pages hardbound with paper jacket (with color illustrations). *"The book is well-written and would make an excellent addition to a primary school library."—India West.*

Nene And The Horrible Math Monster
ISBN 1-879965-02-X

Written by Marie Villanueva and illustrated by Ria Unson. Nene, a Filipino American girl confronts the model minority myth, that all Asians excel at mathematics, and in doing so, overcomes her fears. 36 pages hardbound with paper jacket (with color illustrations). *"The book is engaging and delightful reading, not just for this age group [third grade], but for older school children, and adults as well."—Special Edition Press.*

Blue Jay In The Desert
ISBN 1-879965-04-6

Written by Marlene Shigekawa and illustrated by Isao Kikuchi. This is the story of a Japanese American boy and his family who are interned during World War II. It is the story of young Junior and his Grandfather's message of hope. 36 pages hardbound with paper jacket (with color illustrations).

ONE small GIRL
ISBN 1-879965-05-4

Written by Jennifer L. Chan and illustrated by Wendy K. Lee. Do all Asian Americans look alike? Jennifer Lee is one small girl trying to amuse herself in Grandmother's store and Uncle's store next door, but it's hard when she's not supposed to touch anything. As she goes back and forth between the two stores, Jennifer Lee finds a way to double the entertainment for one small girl in two big stores. 30 pages hardbound with paper jacket (with color illustrations).

Almond Cookies & Dragon Well Tea
ISBN 1-879965-03-8

Written by Cynthia Chin-Lee and illustrated by You Shan Tang. Erica, a European American girl, visits the home of Nancy, her Chinese American friend. In her glimpse of Nancy's cultural heritage, she finds much to admire and enjoy. Together, the two girls learn that the more they share, the more each of them has. 36 pages hardbound with paper jacket (with color illustrations). *"Well crafted. Very stylish for today's America."—The Book Reader.*

Stella: On The Edge Of Popularity
ISBN 1-879965-08-9

Written by Lauren Lee. Stella, a Korean American girl, struggles to be popular at school, even if it means pretending to be what she's not. Stella finds that it's not always easy to be sure just who she's supposed to be. It's especially hard when her parents are always busy working and her grandmother wants her to be a good Korean girl while the other kids at school are typically all-American. 100 pages hardbound with paper jacket.

grub